When I was little, I thought freedom
meant I could eat all the caterpillar cupcakes
I wanted and watch TV for three days
straight. Boy, was I wrong. -Buck

For Josie. Thanks.

BUCK the CHUCK™

The Fight For
FREEDOM

Lynn & Jeff Yelton

FreedomBlossom Press™
freedomblossompress.com

Once upon a time and even right now, unusual heroes have joined the fight for freedom. Buck the Chuck is one of those heroes.

Buck is a woodchuck, a fat, fuzzy fluffball known for chewing and digging and predicting the weather.

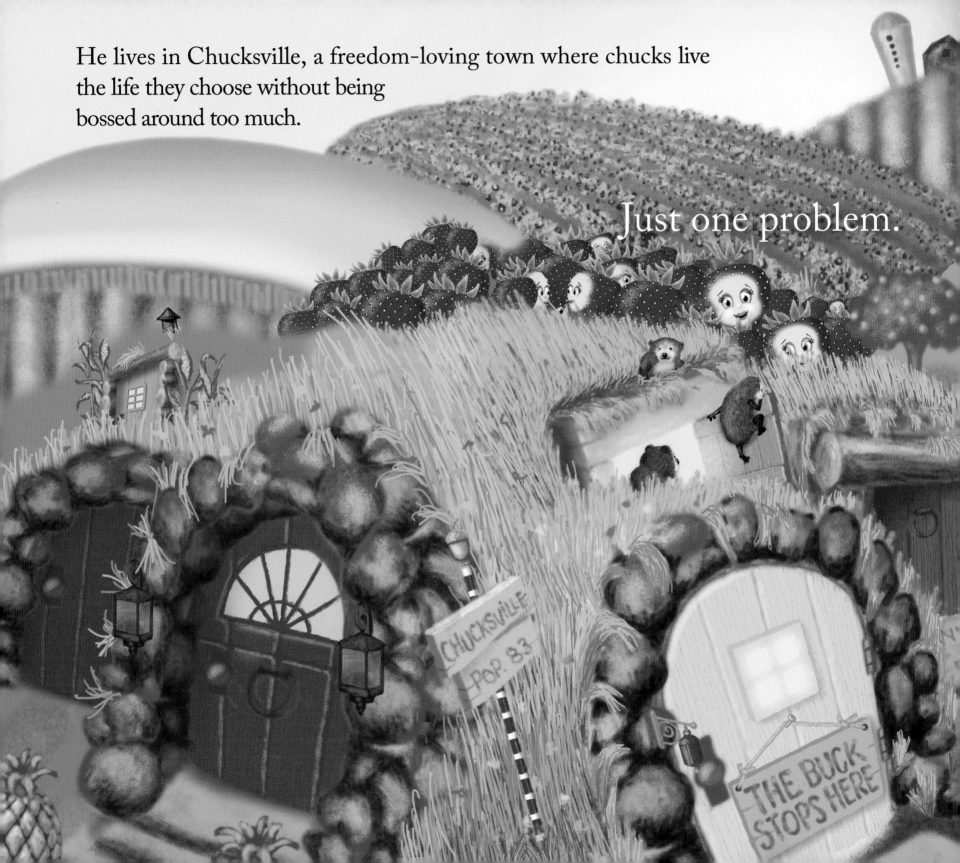

He lives in Chucksville, a freedom-loving town where chucks live the life they choose without being bossed around too much.

Just one problem.

CHUCKSVILLE
Pop. 83

THE BUCK STOPS HERE

KEEP OUT

SWAMPY FOREST
FREEDOM-FREE ZONE

It's **toooo** close to the swampy forest.

That's where the BoozleBoops live—those Lying, Sticky-Fingered, Freedom-Thieving scoundrels!

Bad guy.

One day while reading a scoop by his favorite reporter, Buck was totally gobsmacked! The bad guys were marching toward Chucksville with plans to steal freedom just like they had in the swampy forest!

Freedom THIEVES???

NEWS & THE DAILY HEARSAY
CHUCKSVILLE
TUESDAY
VOL. X NO. 13

ATTACK IMMINENT!
At precisely 7:36 A.M. Monday, a group of sneaky-looking creatures was spotted at the edge of the Swampy Forest by Loretta Chuck. Loretta, who was adjusting the school bell at that very moment, offered the following description: "pirate whiskers, pointy ears, hippopotamus bodies, vicious, slobbering fangs and shocking-pink bowties with a hint of cranberry." The creatures are believed to be the BoozleBoops who stole freedom and its colors from the residents of the Swampy Forest turning the swamp into a wasteland of gray. "Their devious, up-to-no-good expressions told me they were trouble," said Loretta. "That's trouble with a capital 'T.' Con't page 2.

By Maggie, ace reporter, and Jumbo Shrimp

A BOOZLEBOOP
Crafty grin
Evil eye
Snooty snout
Jaunty colors
INVASIVE SPECIES!!

DIRE WARNING FROM EXPERTS!
"Some greedy, know-it-alls who like telling everyone else what to do want your colors! WATCH OUT!" - Tom

This was NOT good news!

CLASSIFIEDS

MISSING: Crayons from large box. All colors except GRAY! Owner cannot fully express herself without freedom to choose colors. Reward offered for safe return. Call 555-1233 if found. No questions asked.

FOUND: Large splat of orange near pond.

WANTED: Big bone (preferably femur) for snacking and burying. Can offer digging and sniffing services in exchange. Call Spike at 555-3321.

TODAY'S WEATHER
Scattered showers with a chance of MOONBOWS

AG FUTURES by Jack
CORN
WHEAT
SOYBEANS

SALE!
NACHOS
Nacho roll-ups!

3 for 1!!
Peach!
Blueberry!
Dandelion!

Suddenly, the sound
of crying chucks filled the air!
Something bad was happening!

Buck dashed to the window. The BoozleBoops—good fish gone bad—crept closer, twirling their twirly mustaches and shifting their shifty eyes.

YIKES,
what should I do?
said Buck to himself
pretty sure he
should hide.

Just at that moment, Buck heard a mysterious **SPLAT!** Something hairy had crash-landed in his living room!

Buck was skeptical but polite.

Meanwhile, the threat of attack kept growing. Freedom was in trouble and Buck needed Thor's help!

LIKE MAGIC Thor sprouted a funky pair of flappers and flew off with his friend to see what freedom looks like.

Darting and zooming and zooming and darting, Thor circled Chucksville while Buck tried to stay calm.

Chucksville was colored bright with the fruits of freedom. There was working and playing and dreaming and digging, plus chucking wood and pondering life's great questions. All the stuff chucks like and are free to do.

Because of freedom, chucks could color their world any way they wanted to— as long as they didn't mess up their neighbors' colors, as some of them did from time to time.

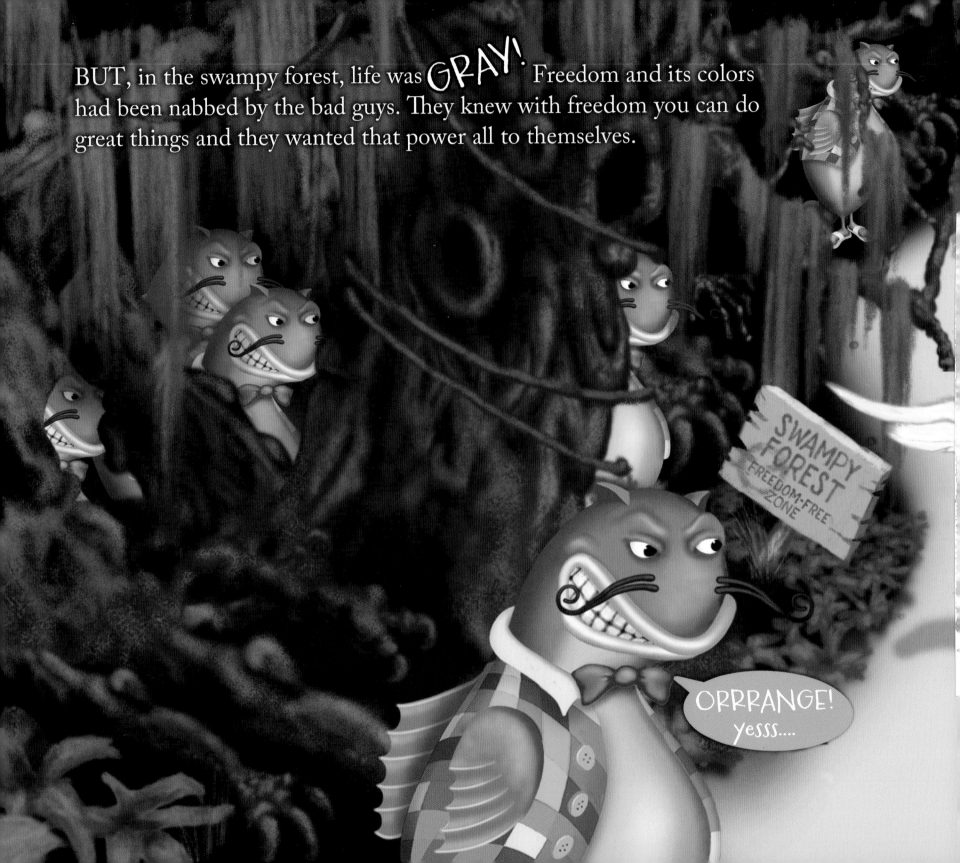

BUT, in the swampy forest, life was GRAY! Freedom and its colors had been nabbed by the bad guys. They knew with freedom you can do great things and they wanted that power all to themselves.

Now, they had plans
for Chucksville!

First they
took RED
from the robin,

then ORANGE
from the orange.

CAFETERIA
ONLY
~~Featuring~~
Brussels Sprouts
✓ Sunday
✓ Monday
✓ Tuesday
✓ Wednesday
✓ Thursday
✓ Friday
✓ Saturday

CRAYONS
CRAYONS
GRAY

Every time we lose some of our freedom, we lose some of our color...until the only choice left is GRAY!

Buck had seen enough.
It was time to stand up for freedom!

In preparation for landing, please make sure your seatbelt is securely fastened and...your foot is not in my eye...

They landed just in time. The BoozleBoops
were turning Chucksville GRAY!

Buck needed to do something! But what? He turned to Thor for advice.
But as fast as Thor had popped in, he popped out!

Yikes!

Buck knew it was all up to him now. Then he remembered Thor's words:

WOW, whoppers for choppers!

THE BATTLE FOR FREEDOM WAS ON!

Mustering all the courage that was muster-able, Buck bared his big, bold teeth and made scary noises that scared even him! He charged the BoozleBoops!

And then it was over.

The battle was done. The chucks had won. And the bad guys were on the run… except for the pails because they didn't have any feet.

One thing was for sure. For now, freedom and its colors were safe thanks to Buck!

Buck fought for freedom even though it was scary. For his courage—and not piddling in the face of danger—his friends surprised him with an awesome costume party!

It was very colorful! Even Leonard.

DID YOU KNOW that woodchuck, whistle pig and groundhog are all names for the same animal?

DID YOU KNOW that a moonbow is a rare, white-colored rainbow that appears at night?

DID YOU KNOW that many people around the world have very little freedom because they live under rulers like kings and tyrants who tell them what they can do and how they can live? These rulers are the enemies of freedom. The United States of America is the only nation in the world founded on the principles of freedom and personal liberties, with government beholden to the people. Our founders–George Washington, John Adams, Thomas Jefferson and others–believed it is freedom that allows us to unleash our full potential. They maintained we are all born with certain God-given, natural rights like life, liberty and the pursuit of happiness, and they established our system of government for the purpose of safeguarding our individual rights. This means we are free to follow our dreams, think our own thoughts, color outside the lines, and work hard to build the type of life we want as long as we don't squelch somebody else's rights in the process. Freedom comes with responsibilities; we are responsible for the choices we make. Sometimes we give up a little of our freedom to help with things like law and order (and parents). Throughout our history, those who have come before us–and even now–have fought to protect freedom so we can have it too.

Stay tuned for Buck and his friends' next adventure in the fight for freedom!

Starring:

BUCK the CHUCK
– our reluctant
but lovable hero

THOR
– Buck's guardian
whistle pig,
in training

MAGGIE
– ace reporter from
*The Daily News &
Hearsay*

JUMBO SHRIMP
– Maggie's feisty
but trusty steed

THE BOOZLEBOOPS
– the bad guys

Book and cover design by Lynn and Jeff Yelton.

BUCK the CHUCK and FreedomBlossom Press are trademarks of Yelton-Kennerly, Inc.

Library of Congress Control Number: 2019900918
ISBN 978-1-7336413-0-2 (paperback)

First edition 2019
Published by FreedomBlossom Press.
Printed and bound in U.S.A.

FreedomBlossom Press

P.O. Box 139, Sherwood, WI 54169
freedomblossompress.com

Freedom is living the life we choose without being bossed around too much.
We are freedom strong!